Some of my favorite childhood memories are centered around Christmas. Fortunately, my parents made sure that we heard the Biblical story of Christmas so that we would know the importance of Christ's birth. For several years, our small-town church set up a live nativity scene complete with animals.

Most grown-ups are familiar with the children's Christmas classic, *The Night Before Christmas*. In a similar manner, this book tells the story of *The Real Night Before Christmas* from the perspective of a little duck who might have been at the stable at Bethlehem long ago.

Make new memories with your child this year with *The Real Night Before Christmas!*

Mike Gay

Cedarmont Kids®

The Real Night Before Christmas
Copyright © 2010 by Cedarmont Music, LLC
Illustrations © 2010 by Cedarmont Music, LLC
Distributed in the United States by Provident-Integrity Distribution,
741 Cool Springs Blvd., Franklin, TN 37067.
Unauthorized duplication prohibited.

Requests for information should be addressed to:
Cedarmont Music, LLC
PO Box 680145
Franklin, TN 37068-0145

Library of Congress Cataloging-in-Publication Data: Applied for
Library of Congress Control Number: 2010912226

ISBN 978-0-9845935-0-7

Mfg. by RR Donnelley, Reynosa Mexico, August 2010 - POCMB100825

The Real Night Before Christmas

By **Mike Gay**

Illustrated by **John Jordan**

'Twas the night before Christmas
and all through the land—
Caesar said, "Take a census,
and tax every man."

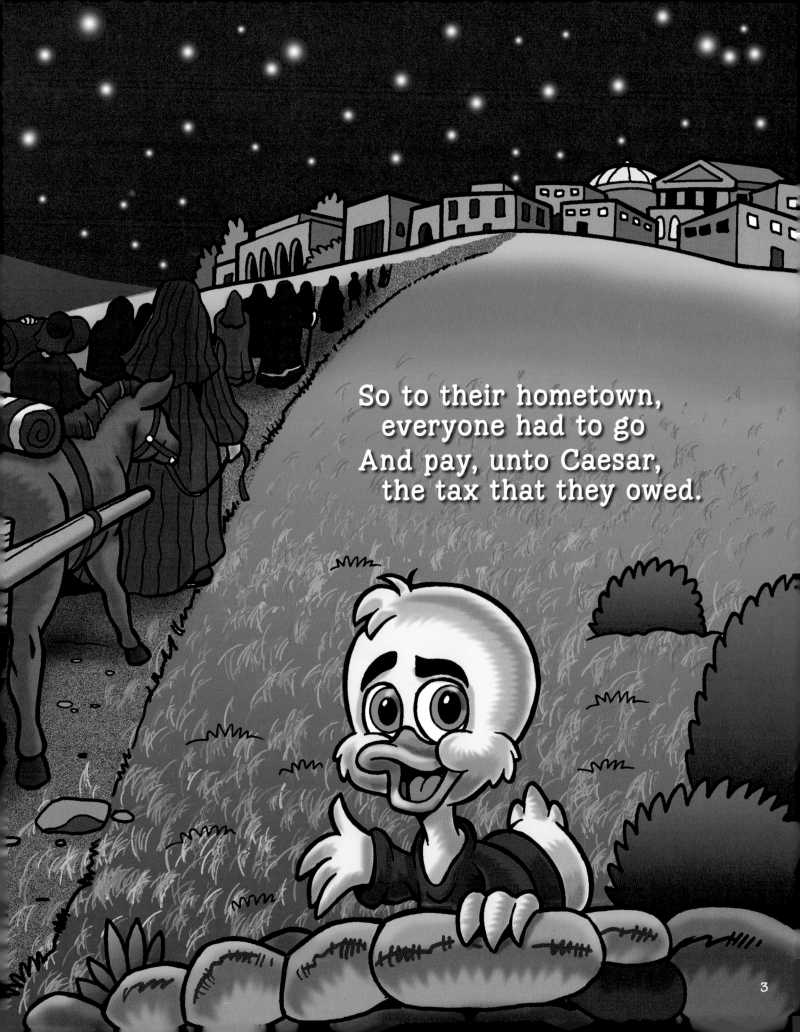

So to their hometown,
everyone had to go
And pay, unto Caesar,
the tax that they owed.

In the town was a stable where the animals stayed;
There was plenty of feed, there was plenty of hay.
The cows and the donkeys were all in their stalls,
And the hens and us ducks made our nests near the wall.

When all of a sudden there arose a great clatter,
I poked up my head to see what was the matter!

11

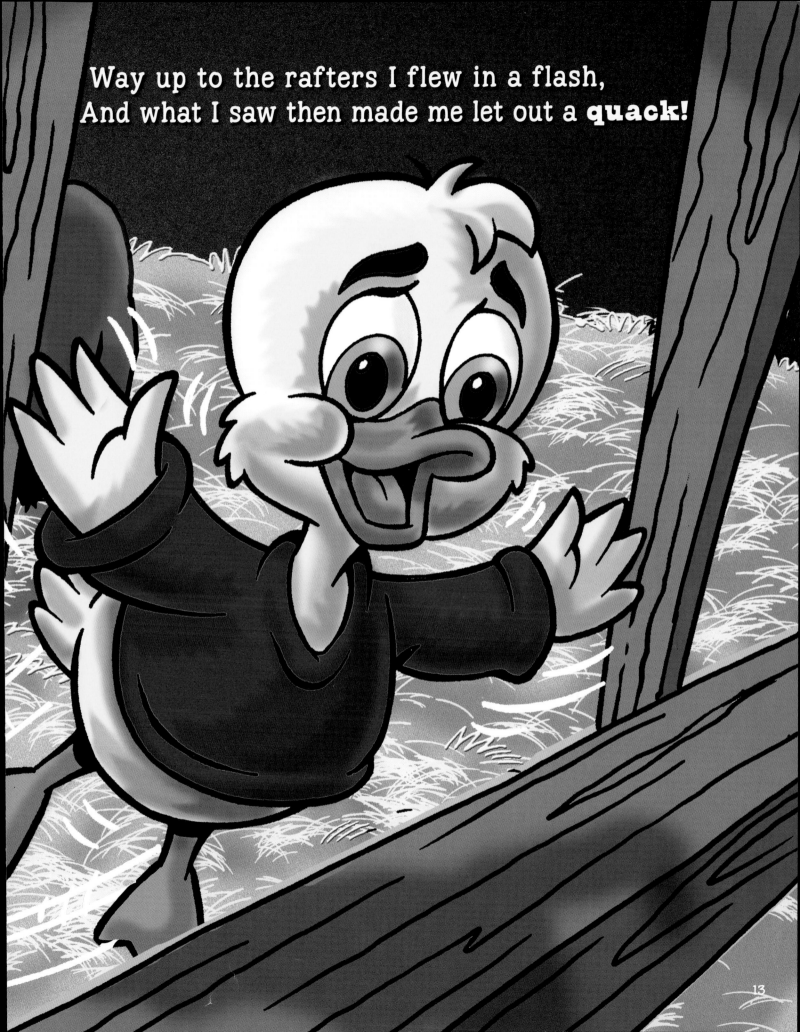

Way up to the rafters I flew in a flash,
And what I saw then made me let out a **quack!**

The sky was so clear, and a big star gave a glow;
Yes, it looked just like mid-day on the city below.

Then what to my little duck-eyes should appear
But a girl on a donkey, with a man walking near?

Then they entered the stable
and rolled out their bed;
There was no other place,
so they slept there instead.

When the baby was born,
    Mary held him so close.
Then she took him and wrapped him
    in swaddling clothes.

And the shepherds were out in the fields nearby;
They were keeping watch over their flock by night.

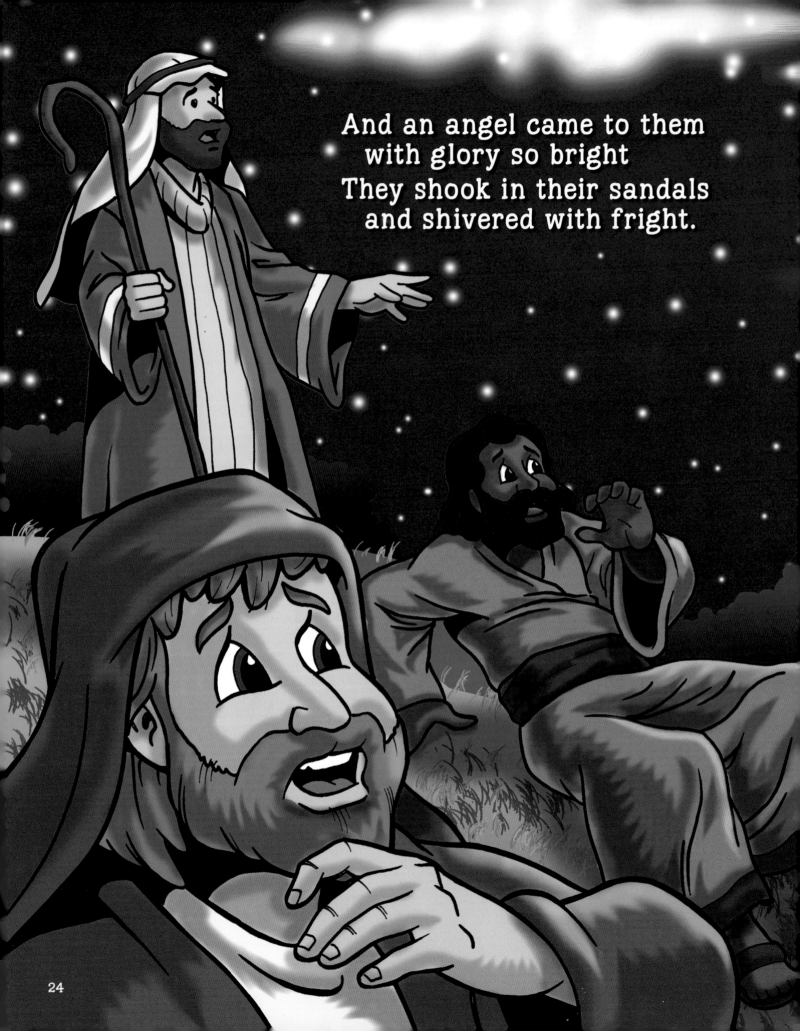

And an angel came to them
with glory so bright
They shook in their sandals
and shivered with fright.

But the Angel said to them,
"Fear not: for behold,
I bring you great tidings
of joy to be told:"

25

"In the city of David, a babe has been born;
He is your Savior, **Christ Jesus**, the Lord!"

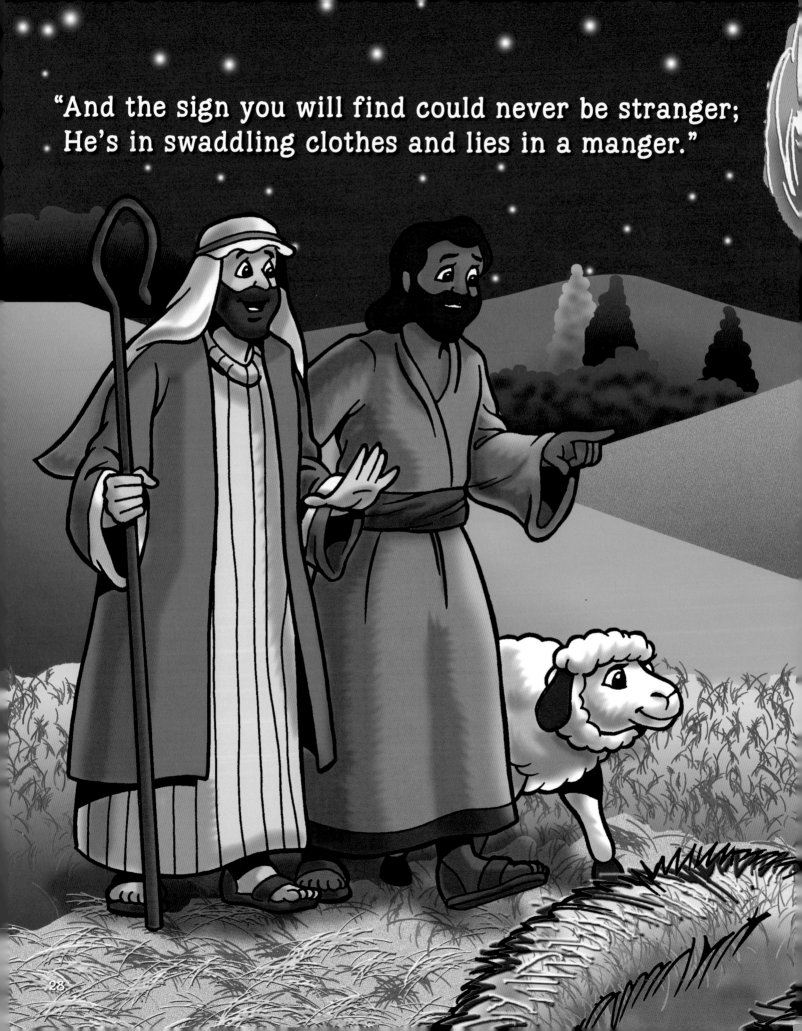

And the heavenly host sang again and again:
"Glory to God! Peace on earth to all men!"

We hope you enjoy *The Real Night Before Christmas*, the newest addition to our product line. With over 20 Million units sold, Cedarmont Kids® has been the top-selling Christian children's music for years. Products include 30 audio CDs in English, 15 CDs in Spanish, 11 full-length DVDs, and several songbooks.

This book was created as a result of our newest CD, **Jingle Ducks**. The audio version of *The Real Night Before Christmas* can be heard on the CD which features 13 Christmas Songs such as *Jingle Bells, Joy To The World, Holly Jolly Christmas, Duck on the Housetop* and others. Kids love the hilarious "duck" voice of Jimmy "Duck" Adkins, and will want to hear this over and over.

Available at Christian Bookstores everywhere!
For more information, visit our website at www.cedarmont.com

Cedarmont Kids® Classics Series
The best songs never go out of style!

With multiple Gold and Platinum certifications, this series features timeless arrangements of classic children's songs.

CD Features: • 15–25 Songs per CD • Split-track versions for sing–along • Lyrics are included • Budget pricing
DVD Features: • 15–25 Songs • Songs repeat in Split-track & Spanish • Lyrics available onscreen as subtitles • Include bonus: Production notes

Cedarmont WORSHIP for Kids
Developing a Heart for Worship in Every Child

Cedarmont's newest series features some of today's best praise and worship songs. Each CD includes 12 songs arranged so that kids can sing them. Separate split-track CDs and songbooks are also available.

CEDARMONT KIDS GOSPEL SERIES
Classic Christian Songs with an upbeat Gospel Sound

FEATURES: • 15-17 Songs per CD • Songs repeat in Split-track for singalong • Lyrics Included • Live-Action DVD available on Gospel Bible Songs

Cedarmont BABY™ Series
Music with a Message They Won't Outgrow!

Recent research indicates that early exposure to instrumental music can help your baby be brighter and happier. With this series, you can stimulate your child's mind and spirit by introducing them to Christian melodies they will treasure forever.

Songbooks

FEATURES: Vocals are arranged with traditional melodies in singable keys with piano parts arranged with the same feel as the recordings, but simplified to be easily playable. A complete guitar chord chart is included.